FOREVER

THE COMPANION
RENZO + LUCIA, BOOK 4

BETHANY-

Published by Bethany-Kris

www.bethanykris.com

ISBN 13: 978-1-988197-97-5

Cover Art © London Miller

Editor: Nina S. Gooden

For all my loves.

CONTENTS

ONE

"You're not listening to me."

"No," Lucia replied, "you're not listening to *me*. And that's the far bigger problem here considering I'm the only gallery in this city that offered to show your work."

Most days, Lucia loved her job as an art gallery owner and curator. Then, she had days like today where she wondered why in the hell she chose this career path at all.

Well, that was partly a lie.

She didn't really *wonder.*

Lucia chose a career in the art world because art was the only thing she found passion in when it came to *work*. It was the one thing she knew she would be able to do for the rest of her life and never become bored. She found art in everything. She looked for it everywhere. She might not be the *artist* who created things, but she was the person who loved the final product and appreciated it the very most.

Still, though, she had times when she wondered why she chose this career, even if she knew every reason. Today was, unfortunately, one of those days.

"Listen, there's no reason why—"

"There are several reasons why I won't meet your demands for this gallery showing," Lucia said. "And if you want, I will repeat them to you, Mr. Tremblay."

"Listen, Luc—"

"Mrs. *Zulla.*"

She almost smiled at the way the man stiffened a bit, standing a little straighter in front of her. And not even because of him, but simply because she liked the way that name came out of her mouth. Years after marrying Renzo, here she was at twenty-nine, and *damn* ... she still loved saying her surname, the one he'd given her.

It was something he'd waffled on. A part of him hadn't wanted her taking the name because of what he'd seen as a stain that covered it. A legacy that wasn't hers to carry; a burden only he should carry alone. Someone had thought to suggest maybe he take her surname, and Lucia would have been just fine with that, too.

Instead, she'd fought for his name.

Who he was.

Renzo Zulla.

That's who she'd met him as all those years ago. That's the man she knew, the one she'd fallen in love with, and the same one who'd proven time and time again that he was absolutely worthy of her the same way she was destined for him. So yeah, she'd taken his name and she wore it with pride. She hoped he did, now, too.

At least, he seemed to.

Leaning back in the white leather office chair that rested behind her glass desk, Lucia waited for a response from the other person in the room. The man—who'd thought coming a couple of feet inside her office while he barked at her about what *he* wanted for his upcoming showing, in *her* gallery, would get him what he wanted— fumed. Some men were like that—didn't appreciate a woman in any position of power, and certainly not one that was above them. In Lucia's business as the owner and director of an art gallery that she'd taken over from her aunt, Kim, a couple of years back, well … it could be even more prevalent.

Plus, art was all about passion.

Artists were *passionate*.

They had a vision.

She got that.

Understood it perfectly fine.

Unfortunately, the vision of the artist didn't always translate to *success*. And that's where she came into play. All those art degrees she'd worked for, and the business one added on top just for good measure, well, that shit wasn't just for decoration. She understood what would make art *sell* in this market. She knew how to put an artist's work on display, and make their name and brand stand out, without them even needing to be in the same room to do it.

"I just think that we should do it *my* way, considering it's my art," Mason said, trying to soften his stance a bit. Maybe so he didn't look as … *arrogant* standing there. Who was she to say? It was too little, too late for her, though, because Lucia saw right through it. "And that is the point of this showing, right? To *show off my art?*"

"No, actually."

"Pardon?"

Lucia smiled. "The point of the showing is to *sell* your art. And if you think having my clientele walk through this place, after it has been turned into some trash heap because it'll *go with the theme*, as you say, then you came to the wrong place to get this done. So, what do you want to do? Sell your art and make money so that someday you can put your entire vision on display the way you want to, or cut your contract with me and go your way? By all means, I will let you make the choice and won't say a word about it otherwise."

It took the man a second.

Then, two.

"I guess, I don't really have a choice, do I?"

"You do—I just gave you two."

Take it or leave it, buddy, she thought.

Lucia understood the man's plight, but he'd gone about this entirely wrong. Had he genuinely been concerned about his vision coming to life as much as possible, then he could have *asked* her if there was something more they could do to the gallery for the upcoming showing. Instead, he'd marched into her office, looking like he'd just rolled out of bed and smelling like he'd spent the night in a bar, with demands as though she were going to fold just because he'd said so.

Hard pass.

Lucia had better things to do.

And money to make.

She loved art.

No doubt about it.

Her respect for art and this business went beyond the pale—she lived for it. Thing was, the only way she could continue to do that was if she made enough money to make it possible. The same thing went for the artists making the art.

They needed money.

Simple as that.

The phone on her desk rang just as Mason looked like he might open his mouth and say something else. If this were another day, one where she had more patience and had spent the night in bed with Renzo, she might have given him the chance to talk. Instead, she waved her hand at the door behind with him with a sharp, "Anything else, take it to my assistant, okay?"

He huffed.

She smiled *again*.

Once she was alone in her office, she picked up the ringing phone. "Lucia here."

"*Dolcezza.*"

That time, her smile was real.

Entirely true.

"Daddy," she greeted, turning her chair away from the desk a bit to stare out the window of her office, where she could enjoy the sight of a bright sky overhead. "What are you up to this afternoon?"

"Coming to see if you might like to clear some time off that *very* busy schedule of yours, actually."

"Excuse me?"

"You never take a break. I am in the city to do some last-minute business before your mother and I take our trip to Bali … and I know Renzo is coming home from Vegas this week sometime, isn't he?"

Yes.

God, she couldn't wait.

She didn't have a clue what job Renzo had been on, but it'd taken him away for almost three weeks. It was unusual for him to be allowed to take his phone and call her when he was on a job, so instead, she was stuck waiting for that call which said he was back in the country. Finally, she'd gotten that today.

He'd be home *soon.*

"He is, yes," she replied.

"So, you'll be tied up with him for a while, won't you? Which means I probably won't get to see you until we get back from our trip."

Her father knew her so well.

A lot like the rest of her family.

"Very possibly," she replied.

"Then, I think you could at least let me take you to lunch before he hides you away."

She had more than enough reasons to say no. Owning her own gallery meant the work never stopped. If it wasn't one thing, then it was another. She also now needed to brief her assistant on the artist who seemed determined to toe every line and work her very last nerve. The less she had to deal with him after today, the better it would be. She had a lot to do, and she really couldn't afford to cancel her next two meetings to have lunch with her dad when she already planned to just take it in her office that day.

But ...

At the same time, she loved her dad.

Missed him, too.

Sometimes, they didn't get enough time together. He never said anything about it one way or another. And she tried not to point it out, either. She never missed a chance to spend her day with her dad.

"How long before you get here?" she asked.

Lucian chuckled. "I am outside with a car running."

Of course, he was.

Lucian knew her well.

"I will be out in two minutes."

"*Perfetto, mia cara.*"

TWO

"Zulla!"

Renzo spun on his heels at the familiar voice calling his name from behind him as he headed through the lower halls of The League. Alessio, a high-ranking member of The League and independent assassin, like Ren, stuck his head out of the knife room. On another day, he might have stopped to have a conversation with the man—he even noticed him when he passed the room—but today, he had other things on his mind.

Better things, really.

No offense to Les.

Alessio arched a brow at the sight of Ren, who was still walking backward and not even stopping at the call of his name.

"Too busy to have a conversation with me or what?"

Renzo laughed, entirely unbothered and knowing Alessio wouldn't be offended. The last few years of Les's life had been kind to him, maybe even softened the guy's fast attitude in a way. Renzo figured settling down and having a couple of kids could do that for a person. "Nah, I uh—"

"Oh, wait, you were on the Bosnia job, weren't you?"

"Yeah, just got back in. The rest of the team is getting in on the next flight coming in. I took the only opening they had on a flight before theirs."

"*Right*," Alessio said, rocking back on his heels. "The wife is waiting for you. I get it."

He bet.

Shit, Alessio had *two* spouses to get back to.

"We'll chat another time, then, yeah?" the guy asked.

Ren nodded. "You know it. Later."

Alessio slipped back into the room he'd come out of and Renzo spun around on his heels, heading deeper into the complex. He walked familiar halls, took the stairs a couple of levels higher, and met up with a few more familiar faces along the way. Of course, none of that stopped him longer than a quick hello before he continued on his way. It didn't take long for him to make it to the office upstairs that Dare rarely left when inside the compound. After arriving back from any job, each member who was independent for The League was required to debrief. It didn't matter if they all had the exact same thing to say.

Policy and all that shit.

You know, if breaking policy meant losing your life and all.

"Renzo," Dare greeted just as Renzo came to stand beyond the entrance of the man's office. The door forever seemed to be open, although Renzo never truly understood why. It seemed dangerous, in a way, but maybe it proved just how much of a danger the man who owned the office was. That, and Dare had access to every single camera within The League's complex. He knew each and every person who came inside, and exactly where they were while within the walls of the place. "Good to see you in one piece, after that one—your phone is on the table. Your wife has been sent a message letting her know you're back in the country."

"Perfect."

"Go ahead and let me know the specifics so you can head out."

A lot of shit had changed at The League for Renzo over the years. He wasn't sure if it was his seniority at the place, despite the fact that he sometimes wondered if he made the right choice in staying as a member. Or was it just the respect that he'd earned over time doing what he did here? But things were different. There was a mutual appreciation all around the board for the people he'd found and had here and he liked that just fine. Part of it, he knew, revolved around the fact that even though Renzo no longer had to be here working, he still was.

Renzo did as Dare requested and briefed the man on the Bosnia job, which had taken three days longer than he'd expected it would. That little time delay had been based on factors that were entirely out of The League's hands because of circumstances. None of which would cause a problem for them. What mattered was that the job was finished successfully. Still, everything had been standard, and the client who'd hired the team would be happy to know that he'd blown open that safe without causing more than a million in damages.

Which meant *more money.*

While he spoke, he headed deeper into the office and picked up his waiting—entirely charged—cell phone from the table in the middle. Dare said nothing as he continued to talk while scrolling through the phone to all the text messages—*three hundred missed ones*, in fact. Mostly from Lucia, and a few from Diego and his sister, likely.

But most came from her.

Lucia.

He smiled, pulling up her thread of messages to go through a few at the very bottom. As she always did, whether he was out of the country or just spending the night at Rose's after being out with Diego for a day, she updated him throughout the day about what was happening or what she was doing with messages.

A *good morning, love you* when the sun rose for her, and a *night, babe, fucking miss you* when she laid her head down on a pillow at night.

But *especially* when he was out of the country, she tended to do it more. It gave him something to look forward to when coming home. He'd sit through her talking about all that he'd missed while he was gone, too.

"And that's all?" Dare asked.

Renzo glanced up from his phone, coming back into the conversation he hadn't really left but wasn't one-hundred percent engaged in. Now that he was back in America, he had too many other important things on his mind.

The job was done.

Successful.

Nothing else mattered but getting home to Lucia.

Like he always promised to.

Forever.

"Yeah, that's it," he said.

Dare nodded, never turning away from the screen covering one entire wall where he watched a sports game. With a wave over his shoulder, he said, "I will be in touch, Ren, look for the final deposit into your accounts."

"Will do."

He was halfway out of the office, and ready to call Lucia and hear her voice for the first time in weeks, when the phone in his hand buzzed with a call. The ringtone that accompanied it had him grinning even though it wasn't his wife calling.

"Diego," Ren greeted, picking up the call, "I just got back, kiddo."

"*Ah*, Ren, don't call me that."

He laughed it off, as he always did. Yeah, Diego *acted* like he didn't like it when his big brother teased him a bit, but Ren knew that in truth, he did. He was the only person Diego had that type of relationship with. Serious but *fun*. He really was the only father the kid knew, even if they were really half-brothers. Diego got both in him.

Someone to be his father when he needed it.

And the big brother he wanted even more.

"Are you back in New York?" Diego asked.

Damn, he wished.

"No, just got back to Vegas, but I am on my—"

"Rose said I can come over, so …"

Ren chuckled. "Buddy, I just got back. I haven't even been home to see Lucia yet, you know?"

"So, when you get back in town, I can come over, right?"

Lord.

He couldn't tell this kid no. Even if he just wanted to spend one night alone with his wife before he got back to his real life, that likely wouldn't happen.

Not that he wanted to tell Diego no, anyway, because he missed his little brother, too. Because for as much as Diego needed his brother, Renzo needed the kid. He was never going to be separated or taken from his brother again.

"You know what? Yeah," Renzo said. "Absolutely, Diego. We'll work it out, okay?"

"Okay, Ren."

He hung up from his brother shortly after and immediately tried to call his wife. The damn thing rang through to voicemail *twice.*

Shit.

Sometimes, she turned it off when she was with clients. He decided *whatever.* After all, it'd been a while since he'd surprised her. So, why not?

THREE

"Thanks," Lucia told the cab driver.

He handed her card back over with a nod. "Have a good evening, ma'am."

"You, too."

Stepping out of the vehicle into the quiet Brooklyn street, Lucia didn't take much time to admire the sight of her home or the relief at the fact she was finally *here* after a very long day. Instead, she headed past the gate that led up to the brownstone's steps, already pulling out her keys and readying to unlock the door.

She didn't need the keys, though.

The door was unlocked.

That might have made her pause, but when she pushed open the door, the thing she hadn't been expecting to greet her was the noise. Well, it didn't so much greet her as it just filled the space entirely.

Music blasting from the surround sound system. Something that sounded like a game being played accompanied the tunes. Laughter—*masculine*—followed the noise from two distinct people, both of which she recognized. They made her smile grow larger as she kicked off her shoes and discarded her coat to a waiting hook before heading farther into the place.

She swore every light between the entrance and down to the living room had been turned on, when she was *positive* she had turned them off before leaving that morning. It had become a habit. She had to do her own part to save the environment and whatnot.

On another day, this much noise in her house wouldn't be unusual. When Renzo was home, he always had to be doing something. Rarely did he sit back and relax. Typically, he liked to have everything on while he did it, too—music, the TV or whatever. Sometimes, he had a person or two over just because he enjoyed the company. More often than not, it was his little brother.

The only time she could quiet that man and his mind was at night. When it was just the two of them together in bed, or the bath … alone. *That's* when he settled, and she loved being one of the few things that could bring him back down to earth. She gave him peace, and he reminded her of exactly why she loved her life.

Because he was in it.

She passed by a familiar bookbag in the hallway, the contents, which included a textbook and a tablet, slightly spilling to the floor where its owner left it to stay. She didn't even care that it made a mess because that bookbag meant one thing and one thing only.

Diego was here.

Which meant so was Renzo.

She was right, too.

Lucia leaned in the entryway to the living room, smiling at the sight that waited for her there. Renzo threw his hands wide, his back turned to her as his character on the screen from the game he currently played with his fourteen-year-old brother, Diego, was blown sky-high from whatever weapon the teenager used on him.

Diego took his moment to shine, doing a little victory dance on the spot while at the same time, mocking his brother. Renzo, on the other hand, wasn't a sore loser, and she swore he only kept the damn game system around just because Diego loved it so much. Because while he was good at it, he also didn't get nearly enough time to play and enjoy it the way he wanted.

"*Ha!* Told you, Ren. You *suck.*"

"I do not. It's just … been a fucking while, yeah? Don't get cocky. We're going another round."

The two brothers continued their teasing, and Lucia stayed back to watch them, happy in her spot. They wouldn't mind a bit if she joined them, but she figured they needed at least a couple of more minutes without her in the middle, not that either of them ever complained about her presence.

Yeah, she would definitely have liked to have the night alone with Renzo, seeing as how she figured that he wouldn't be getting back until at least tomorrow, but at the same time … well, she never minded having to share his time and attention.

At least, not with Diego.

Ren had priorities.

They became hers, too.

That was love.

And *life.*

Their life, anyway.

Besides, she loved Diego more than she could explain. It had been a privilege for her to watch the boy grow into a young man these past few years. Not to mention, being able to see Renzo help Diego become who he was just starting to be.

She couldn't ask for more.

They were *so* lucky.

After everything, they still had this.

All this love.

Just as Diego started clicking buttons on his remote to bring the game back to a restart, Renzo turned to grab something on the couch. That's how he noticed Lucia standing in the doorway. For a brief moment, the rest of the world ceased to exist when their gazes met. Or it just stopped turning, but hey, she liked that fine.

It was him and her again.

He was safe.

Home.

Here with her.

"Hey, you," he murmured.

She smiled. "Hey, yourself. Were you trying to surprise me?"

"Maybe. Did it work?"

"Absolutely, Ren. I thought you wouldn't be home until tomorrow."

"Yeah, well … pulled some strings. Diego wanted to come over, too, so—"

"I don't mind."

He gave her another one of those blinding smiles. The kind that still made her stomach twist with butterflies and had her chest growing tight. And when he winked at her, while his brother's back was turned so the kid couldn't see it, she swore the heat he caused shot right down to the spot between her thighs that had gone without this man for far too long.

Yeah.

She missed Ren like nobody knew.

Always did.

"Hey, Lucia," Diego called.

"Hey, buddy."

"Wanna game?"

"Yes, another person to kick my ass," Renzo grumbled. "Stupid, that I do this shit in real life but can't manage to beat it on the game. This shit is rigged."

Lucia laughed, but didn't hesitate to cross the room and pick up the third controller on the coffee table. "You just need to get in your groove, that's all."

"When do I ever get the time anymore?"

That wasn't a lie.

As Diego began the process of restarting and adding a third player to the game, Renzo leaned in to grab Lucia, as she was close enough for him to do it. He pulled her in to his side, and the moment his lips touched down to hers, her world *finally* tilted back to its proper axis. Soft at first, the sweep of his lips against her own stayed gentle for just long enough to get her to open for him. And then he was *really* kissing her, taking away her breath all over again and driving her crazy at the same damn time.

How long had it been?

Too long.

"Missed you," she whispered against his lips.

"Too much, babe. Love you, huh?"

She smiled when he kissed her again. "Forever, Ren."

FOUR

"Okay," Lucia said, huffing as she pushed up from the couch and rested the controller on the coffee table. She didn't know how the two of them could continue to stand to play their game because after a couple of minutes, she was ready to sit her ass *down*. Which she had done, but now she really needed a break. The two of them could play for hours, if they were really into it, but she wasn't like them. "That's enough of getting my butt beat, thank you very much."

Diego's laughter colored the room.

Renzo smirked her way—the *ass*. And she only called him that because he looked damn good, even when he was gloating. Because yeah, it was just like she'd said earlier. He needed to get back into the groove of his game. He was always crap when he first picked up the controller again after leaving it for too long, and then he went right back to beating all of them at the game.

Although, Diego gave Renzo a good run for his money.

"Anybody want drinks?" she asked.

"Water, thanks," Diego mumbled, already restarting the game and trying to take a cheap shot at his brother when Renzo didn't turn his attention right back to the screen. Not that his attempt worked. "Dammit, Ren!"

Renzo had pressed the pause button just as Diego's character came up behind his brother on the screen. "Watch your mouth." Then, to her, he added, "And I'm good, babe, thanks."

Sure.

She bet he wanted a beer. Maybe a blunt. Or a good shot of whiskey, but he was always careful whenever Diego was near. Given their family history of addiction, not to mention the fact that Diego had been born addicted to whatever his mother's vice had been at the time to use, the kid had a higher statistic for things like drug use or worse, full-on addiction. It'd taken an incident the year before—with Diego getting mixed up in a crowd of boys who had the police bringing him home one night—for Ren to put a stop to it all.

Ren took a lot of steps to make sure his brother didn't see him drinking. Or smoking a joint before he went to bed. The kid didn't even see Ren carrying around a pack of cigarettes. Was it all a little much?

Maybe.

All that shit Renzo made sure his brother didn't see him doing was still out there in the world. There was no way for them to control and protect Diego from seeing it all whenever he left his house, went to school, or hung out with his friends. So, they basically hoped that the example they all set forth for Diego was enough to allow him to make the right choices when he was faced with those things.

Truth was, Diego looked up to his brother like nobody else would ever understand. He'd always been the kid's hero, even after it wasn't *cool* for Ren to be that anymore. That didn't make a difference to the fact Diego regularly looked to his brother first as a role model. So, if

Ren did something, it must be good enough for him to do, too.

If Ren didn't stop doing something altogether that wasn't the best influence, then he made sure his brother didn't see him doing it at all.

Was it easy?

No.

Fun?

Certainly not sometimes.

Ren still stuck to it, though.

She respected that.

It was her turn, then, to wink at him before she turned and headed for the kitchen. She was just pulling Diego's bottle of water from the fridge, the condensation slicking her fingertips, when Renzo came up behind her.

God.

He could be silent when he wanted to be.

Sometimes, it freaked her out.

And at the same time, she *still* always knew when he was there. That was why it unsettled her; she could know he was there, but not *hear* him. Through his scent; his presence; the way he affected her, just by being close.

She hoped that never changed for them.

Ever.

"I've got like thirty seconds," he murmured in her ear.

That was all she heard before his lips grazed the side of her throat and he yanked her away from the fridge. Just as quickly as her feet had been on the ground, he lifted her to sit on the counter facing him. The bottle of water was forgotten to the counter while she focused on her husband. He didn't even have to ask, she just widened her thighs to let him step in between her legs—she was grateful for her choice in pants that morning. A black material that looked classy but had just enough stretch to *move*.

And it was just thin enough to let her feel the hard length of him pressing against her pussy in the best way. It made her want to grind on him and get what she wanted the very most. Not that now was the best time for that, but it didn't seem to matter to her because she pushed back against him to get more.

His fingers found her thighs, curving over the muscles before flexing tightly as he closed the distance between them for a hard kiss that had her aching inside. It was nothing like the sweet, but still *hot*, kiss from earlier. Because there was nothing sweet about the way he kissed her like he was two seconds away from dragging her upstairs to bed.

And damn, she wanted that.

Except …

"Ten seconds," he muttered against her lips, pulling away just slightly.

"Before?"

"Diego figures out we're in here doing *this*."

Ah, right.

Diego was at a funny age. He noticed girls, likely had less than innocent thoughts, and was like every fourteen-year-old boy who needed to quickly learn how to do his own laundry, lest his older sister kick him out for not doing so.

At the same time, he wasn't very fond of seeing any grossly public displays between his older brother and Lucia. At least, not moments like *these*.

Renzo stepped back quickly from Lucia, giving her far too much room to breathe as he cleared his throat right before Diego called out, "You better not be—"

"We're *not*," Renzo called back dryly.

It wasn't a lie.

Technically.

Lucia shook her head, laughing softly under her breath. "How long do you think this stage is going to last, huh?"

"You want an honest answer?"

She kind of did.

"Yeah."

"Long enough for him to have sex for the first time. Then, he'll *really* get it. What all this fuss is about. Why he's got raging hormones. Why he wakes up with a morning—"

"That's enough, thanks."

Renzo shrugged. "All part of being a teenage boy. Maybe it's easier on him because he's got lots of guys around him to answer questions when he gains up enough courage to ask, but for me? Man, that part of growing up fucking sucked. Part of him still thinks some shit is gross, while other parts figure ... it might be kind of awesome. He's gotta figure it out."

"I guess one good thing is he isn't having sex yet, right?"

"I mean, we'll see how long that lasts. He knows what to do, either way."

Right.

Because he had Ren for that.

Even if it was awkward.

Renzo stepped forward again, but still somehow managed to keep a slightly respectable distance between them. At least now she couldn't feel his erection driving between her thighs while his tongue slashed against hers. She liked both, honestly, but this was easier for *talking*.

"So, you had a rough week, huh?" he asked.

Her brow furrowed. "Pardon?"

"Your week. Probably a bit longer than you expected it to be."

All at once, Lucia finally understood what he was getting at. All those texts of hers, which she'd sent to him while he was away on his assignment. Keeping him updated with everything, from the fact that the coffee shop she went to every morning ran out of her favorite donuts before she could get one, to the difficult client toward the end of the week.

Instead of replying to his statement about her week—hell, it didn't even matter anymore with him here—she said, "I love you, Ren."

And she did.

More than he would ever know.

She didn't know how to explain a love like this. Something this consuming and perfect … because nothing else about life was perfect. Except them.

And this.

Renzo smiled. "Love you, too."

"But yes, I do think I might need a vacation."

"I could do that for you."

Lucia rolled her eyes. "It was a joke. I don't have time for—"

"What if time was made for you instead?"

She gave him a look.

He *looked* right back at her.

"Don't tempt me."

"Okay," he said, leaning in to press a soft kiss to her lips before he continued on with, "then no temptations. But we'll see what I can do."

"Mmhmm."

"Come on, Ren!"

"The prince calls," he muttered, kissing her once more.

"Keep pretending that you don't like it, then."

A shrug fell from his shoulders as he stepped away from her with that sexy, playful grin of his right back in place. "Listen, I gotta do what I gotta do for this pride of mine."

"Right, right."

God.

She loved that man.

FIVE

"So, did the fourteen-year-old cramp your style last night or …?"

Lucia laughed at Renzo's sister's suggestion as she moved from the smaller illuminated table to the bigger one with an art print in her hand. She needed more space to do what she needed to do. Setting the print to the table and grabbing her magnifying glasses, she answered Rose back with, "You know I don't mind Diego staying the night."

"Yeah, but Ren just got home, right? How long was he gone?"

"Three weeks this time."

"*Right*, so again …"

"I promise I don't mind. We had fun. He passed out on the couch after I filled him full of soda—"

"You did *not* give him soda."

Lucia barked out a laugh. "No, I didn't."

"Good. Swear the kid's fucking addicted to the shit."

"And he asked when Ren was going to take him to see that show … the uh, the car one he's talked about for the last year."

"Are you asking *me*? Because as long as the car works and takes me from point A to point B, I am a happy girl."

Lucia shook her head and pulled the glasses from her eyes to blink over at the phone resting on the table where she had it set on speaker for this conversation. "Anyway, that's coming up, so you might want to get all the details hammered out with Ren."

"Will do. Thanks again, huh?"

"You know I love that kid."

"Yeah, I do. Let me get back to this painting."

"Mmhmm. Are you ever going to let me have a showing for you or what?"

"Someday," Rose joked.

She didn't know if she believed it or not, but she wasn't going to push. Some artists just had their own way of doing things. To be honest, Rose had carved out her own path and name in the art world without much help from anyone else. Plus, there was that whole *don't mix family and business thing.*

It might be better if they didn't work together.

Either way, she was proud of Rose.

Absolutely.

"Later, Lucia."

"You, too."

With the phone call ended, Lucia went back to her work of surveying an art print that she was supposed to find a buyer for, after a client decided it was no longer needed for his personal collection. Which didn't make that much sense to her, considering the piece originally sold for over twenty thousand American dollars.

And now, it was worth *more.*

But whatever.

He wanted to sell it; she'd sell it.

That was part of her job.

Lucia was so lost in her work that she didn't even hear the buzz of her intercom, which signaled her assistant at the front of her gallery was calling through for whatever reason. In fact, she stayed so focused on the print in front of her that the only thing to drag her attention away from it was the sound of a familiar voice echoing down the hall.

"Nah, it's fine, I'll just go back and get her."

She looked up from the print, pulling the glasses from her eyes, in just enough time to watch a gorgeous sight walk through the doorway of one of her back offices. Of course, Renzo looked good. He always did.

But when he threw on a leather jacket?

A pair of ripped jeans?

Combat boots she loved?

Yes.

It was like he walked back in time and she was staring at that boy she'd met on the streets of Brooklyn all over again. And she truly loved nothing more than that feeling of nostalgia.

He closed the door behind him, giving her a sly grin as he did so. "What are you doing back here?"

"Working—like always."

"Mmhmm. You got five minutes for me or what?"

"Always."

Just to prove her point, she reached over and turned the table off—so the light dimmed entirely—before setting the print aside, too, for safe keeping.

By the time she turned around to face Renzo again, ready to ask him what was up because she was sure he said he would be visiting with Rose today, there he was. Right there behind her, already reaching for her and closing all the distance between them in a blink.

His kiss took her breath away.

His hands grabbing to her waist had her moaning.

"Didn't get to do this last night," he murmured against the column of her throat, "so I figured I *better* make time for it today."

"Oh, my *God*."

"Yeah, you're gonna be saying that a lot."

It took him all of a blink to lift her from the floor and twist around to set her to the closest flat, sturdy surface. Which just happened to be the illumination table she thankfully hadn't been using for that very expensive art print. He bunched her skirt up around her waist, his hand slipping between her thighs to grab her panties and rip them away from her body.

She couldn't widen her legs fast enough because he helped, those strong fingers of his digging into her thighs hard enough to make her moan.

"Wet for me?" he asked.

Lucia licked along the line of her bottom lip, replying, "You know all you have to do is be near to get me fucking wet for you, Ren."

And he did know that.

What she knew was that he fucking *loved it*.

"Fuck, yes, that's what I wanted to hear. And people wonder why I miss you so fucking much when I'm gone. They don't know what kind of woman I got here, huh?"

"Shame."

"Fuck 'em."

Lucia laughed, but it was quickly swallowed by his lips finding hers again for another bruising kiss that would certainly ruin her makeup … but *fuck*, she couldn't find it in herself to care in that moment.

"God, I missed you," she breathed into his kiss.

Renzo's laughter coated her in the most sinful and delicious way. Especially because while his dark amusement mixed in with his pleasure, his cock filled her in one hard thrust. He had her flat to the table in seconds, hands slipping under the stretchy fabric of the top of her dress to splay against her stomach as he started a rhythm that would have her flying in no time at all.

He knew what worked best for her body.

How to get her so high, so fucking fast.

And after he'd gotten her off, she knew he would then take his time to drive her crazy before he made her fly one more time. Just because he loved to see her high off him.

Like a drug.

"Jesus Christ," Lucia mumbled against her palm, "you do know I've got a meeting in like … twenty minutes, right?"

That tempting, husky laughter of his filled the room again. His pace never faltered even once as he fucked her closer and closer to an orgasm with every goddamn thrust.

"Oh, no … I just had your next *week* cleared, Lucia."

Her gaze flew open.

He smirked above.

"What?"

"Exactly what I just said, babe. Time for a break. *Now, come.*"

She did.

God.

She loved this man.

Entirely.

SIX

At one point in his life, Renzo thought there would never be a time when he walked into Lucian Marcello's house, and have it feel welcoming to him like a home should. And yet, with years put between their wrongs, time spent respecting each other for more things that were good around them, and a mutual love between them in Lucia, Lucian's home felt like one of the most welcoming places he'd ever been to.

And more often than not, when Renzo needed that fatherly figure in his life that he still didn't have in anyone else, he went to Lucian. He didn't know when it'd happened, or why he'd started crossing that bridge with his father-in-law, but he did it and he couldn't find a single reason to regret it, either.

Lucian came around the corner of the kitchen entry as Renzo entered the man's house, already hearing Jordyn Marcello's laughter drifting from somewhere behind the man. He wasn't privy to whatever joke Lucian had told his wife before their guest arrived, but he didn't feel like he needed to know, either.

Something else Renzo had come to learn about Lucian?

He loved one thing the *very* most.

His wife.

And the man he became around that woman, in private when he

thought no one could see, was someone the outside world never got to see. Their children did, sure, but no one else.

And when he did see Lucian share those moments of affection, Renzo never said a word. But it did make him respect Lucia's father more to know there was a woman in his life who made him just as *crazy in love* as the rest of them, really.

"You owe me and my wife *big time* for this one," Lucian said, giving him a wag of his finger. "Jordyn's been planning this thing to Bali for months now."

"I know, I know—"

"And I know you appreciate it!" Jordyn shouted from the kitchen.

Lucian rolled his eyes. "Come on, woman, I'm fucking trying to make him at least *think* he could owe us for it."

Renzo just shook his head. "No, I do. I really appreciate this. Turns out you can't actually plan a whole vacation in a day, no matter how hard you try or what amount of cash you say you're willing to pay. So, yeah, I appreciate you letting me do this."

"So, you're good, then?" Lucian asked him.

Renzo shrugged. "Just a few last-minute details."

"Ah."

"I need to get some shit packed, but without, you know, *people* finding out. So, I was wondering if maybe Jordyn could—"

Lucia's mother's answer came fast in reply. "I can get that done for you, Ren!"

He laughed. "Well, I guess there's one detail figured out."

Lucian nodded. "And one more for you—thank my brother's wife, because it's Catrina's jet."

"Got it. So, I've got like an hour to get back to the city before her spa appointment is over. Is that going to be possible—"

"No worries," Jordyn said, coming around the corner of the kitchen entryway to join her husband in the hallway with Renzo. "I'm leaving right now. I'll get her all packed up and send the bags to the strip with a driver. He'll be there and it'll all be loaded before you even arrive. Don't worry, it will go off without a hitch. She's going to appreciate this."

Renzo blew out a hard breath.

Fuck.

He hoped so.

Lucia deserved this.

So did he.

For once in his life, literally, everything just wanted to align to make it happen. Along with the generosity of Lucian and Jordyn Marcello, given the Bali trip had originally been theirs. They were kind enough to give it to their daughter. Who was he to fuck with the stars, and all that shit?

Besides … Lucia had said she needed a vacation, hadn't she?

"Have fun," Lucian told him, "and no worries, John will check in with Diego to keep an eye on him, huh?"

"Thanks."

Yeah.

A lot of shit had changed.

Like now?

Renzo had a family.

He'd had a small one before, sure, and he loved his brother and sister more than anyone would ever know. But Lucia gave *them* people, too. More big brothers to watch Diego's back. Mother figures who taught them how to cook or answered late-night questions about sick kids. Male role models who were actually *there*.

Renzo might not need those things at his age. And maybe neither did Rose, in some ways.

But he and Rose couldn't be *all those things* to Diego, all the time. They were humans doomed to fail sometimes, but Lucia gave them a family in hers that really stepped it up when it counted.

He wouldn't give that up for the world.

• • •

"Hey, Ren!"

"Diego," Renzo said back, "did you ace that test or what, man?"

"You know I did."

Renzo chuckled. "Better have."

His brother's sigh echoed throughout the speakers of the Maserati he'd bought for himself as a gift the year before. The first time he'd *ever* allowed himself such an extravagant gift without the usual guilt that accompanied it. The memory of being dirt poor was never going to leave Ren, and, fuck yeah, he still sometimes thought he wasn't worthy of the life he now had.

Just how it was.

Not that he intended to give it up.

Ever.

"Told you I *would*," Diego replied.

"I'm joking. Knew you were gonna kill it. So, hey, listen … I know I said maybe this weekend we could do something, but you know how I say sometimes we gotta take care of us first, instead of everybody else? Be a little selfish sometimes, so then we can go back to being the people everybody needs us to be?"

"Yeah, of course."

Renzo smiled to himself, the miles on the highway coming at him faster and faster as he approached the city limits. Twenty minutes before Lucia's spa appointment ended, and he *had* to be there to pick her up because it was meant to be a *no stress* day before he really finished out her surprise.

"All right, well, Lucia and I gotta do that. We need to take some time to just be us, away from everything else. It's been a long time since we could do that. So, I know I said we'd try for something this weekend, but—"

"Yeah, it's okay, Ren. Next weekend, then?"

"Absolutely, kiddo."

"*Ren.*"

He laughed. "You know you still like it when I call you that, Diego. And *buddy*, too."

"Mmm."

"Anyway, just … promise me you'll stay out of trouble, huh?"

It took his brother a second.

Then, two.

Finally, Diego said, "I disappointed you when I got in trouble last year. Was worse than when you were mad that time, 'cause I lied about that party after baseball. That really fucking sucked, Ren, so I'm not gonna do it again. Just so you know, and all."

"Yeah?"

"Yeah, Ren."

"I just ... you know I want you to have *every* chance that I didn't and more, right?"

Like Diego was his own fucking kid.

Because he basically was.

Renzo *raised* this kid for most of his life.

"Oh, and tell Lucia to have fun," Diego said, "guess I'll call Tessa and see what she's doing."

He cleared his throat, knowing exactly who Tessa was in Diego's life.

"Be safe, huh?"

"I *know.*"

"Just ... I don't mean it to put you on the spot. Like, I think it's gonna happen with you and her because I know what you told me. But it doesn't have to be *right now* for me to remind you of this stuff, okay? Remember everything I've told you, yeah?"

"I do, Ren."

Yeah, he knew.

Still, he worried.

Because that's what people who loved you did.

"Okay, I gotta hit the gas a little harder here or I'll miss Lucia coming out of the spa—she thinks it's gonna be a driver to take her home, but it needs to be me."

"All right, Ren. Love you."

Still cool to say that, he guessed.

"Love you, too, buddy."

SEVEN

"Here's your tea, Mrs. Zulla, and when you're ready to leave, your driver is waiting outside for you."

Still wrapped tightly in the silk robe provided by the spa, Lucia felt appropriately buffed, shined, and *pampered*. From the bottoms of her toes to the very top of her head, her body had never been more relaxed than it currently was. She had to give Renzo credit for knowing what she needed, and right where to send her to get it done.

"Did you enjoy the treatments?" the blonde woman asked, gathering the small plates next to Lucia's chair that had held pastries.

"More than you know."

The woman grinned. "Oh, trust me, I know. Sometimes, we all need one of these days. And I am sure you deserved it."

"I *will* be back."

"Well, no one here will complain about that."

She bet not.

Hell . . .

This place probably ran Renzo a couple thousand dollars, easily. From the mud bath to the honey wrap. Then the heat capsule where everything but her head had been closed into an egg-shaped, pod-looking thing. Steam cleaned out every pore in her body and sucked all that bad shit out.

The dirt.

Her stress.

Whatever.

It had taken it all away, and she still thought her feet floated above the floor. It really spoke to the spa's abilities to make a person forget about the outside and whatever had brought that person running here to make it all go away. Next time she came, if Renzo didn't join her, then she was certainly bringing one of her cousins or sisters.

Or all of them.

They all deserved a day here, surely.

"Your driver said no rush on finishing up," the woman said before heading out of Lucia's private room.

"Thank you."

She did exactly that, too. Took her time to finish the Earl Grey tea, which was her favorite, and only then did she finally shed the silk robe to get dressed in the clothes that waited, folded, on the table next to the chair. When she finally left the room and headed to the waiting room of the spa, the women behind the front desk waved her goodbye.

Distracted by the kind women and wondering when she might be able to sneak back here, Lucia didn't even notice who her *driver* was, who had apparently been waiting for her outside. His low whistle, however, had her spinning around fast to face him where she found the sexiest sight leaning against a familiar, black Maserati.

Renzo.

Damn.

And he loved that car.

Looked so good on it, too.

She didn't expect him to be standing there, considering it was *him* who had told her that another person would pick her up and take her home after this little spa day of his. And despite the fact he'd told her that her entire schedule for the *week* had been cleared, he'd refused to explain further on that topic.

"Look at you, huh? They have you glowing, babe."

Lucia grinned. "You think?"

"Should this be a regular thing?"

She didn't even have to think about it. "Yes, yes it should."

Renzo flashed her with a blinding smile. "Will do."

"Back home?" she asked, coming closer until she could grab the hand that he held out for her. "Or do you have something else planned?"

He winked. "You know me so well. *Definitely* something else. Get in the car—we gotta head out of the city."

"To where?"

"You'll see."

This man was lucky she loved surprises.

• • •

"Ren—"

It was like he could hear the concern in Lucia's voice as she finally recognized where they were, and what the private air strip meant.

Not to mention, the damn jet at the end of the runway looked as though it were on standby and ready to fly.

"Let me talk," he said, never once taking his gaze away from the window while he navigated the Maserati down the long strip, "and then we'll see how you feel, okay?"

She passed him a look.

He still kept his stare on the road.

Dammit.

She loved this man, but she didn't know if she liked this idea of his very much, considering everything that she was now seeing.

"Fine, talk," she said.

"Six days in Bali—a private residence with maids, a cook, and everything. There's even a damn waterfall in the back, Lucia, and a pool that has one glass wall, so it looks like the water just drops off all of the sudden. Can you imagine the views? There'll be no working, nobody bothering you or me, and time for us to get back to what's important here. Tell me that doesn't sound fucking amazing."

"That's my mother and father's trip."

"No, it's ours because they decided to give it to us to use. Don't feel guilty about that—we're just going to pay them back times a hundred for their anniversary or something, okay? So, six days in Bali, *think about it.*"

She sighed.

That did sound lovely.

Perfect, really.

Still, she had to think about everything else she had going on, too.

Life couldn't be as simple as Lucia just packing up her shit and heading out of town for almost an entire week. Even Renzo had to know that, but his next words made it seem like he had all those bits figured out, too.

"Nothing on your schedule was so important, according to your *assistant*—you know, that person you hire to take care of these things for you and be aware of this shit—that it couldn't be moved. Oh, and that showing you have for the artist? It's not for another two weeks, and since I know damn well it's been a major source of stress for you, it would be good to get some time away from it."

"But—"

"Not done, Lucia."

She pressed her lips together, trying to hide her smile. She *loved* that somehow, he'd managed to pull this together for her in a day. How, she didn't know.

"Your aunt, Kim, is going to handle the gallery for the week," Renzo added.

He pulled the car to a stop a good fifty meters away from the private jet—she recognized the plane well enough because it belonged to her other aunt, Catrina. In the driver's seat, Renzo turned to face her with a grin and his eyebrows raised expectantly.

"Your ma packed the bags for us. They're already waiting on the jet. The gallery will be handled. John is going to keep an eye on Diego. Your father will keep everyone else in line."

Lucia laughed lightly. "Of course."

"So, what do you say? Are we going to Bali? You did want a

vacation."

"I was *joking.*"

"Didn't really take it that way, babe."

God.

This man.

She loved him so much.

And right then, all she wanted to do was climb across the front seats of the Maserati and show him just how much she loved him. Which she was sure Renzo would love, too, but chances were … they needed to get on that plane.

"How did you do all this in a day?"

He shrugged. "Money can do anything. That, and a lot of hope, luck, and generosity from your parents."

Right.

She had another thought, then.

Renzo *rarely* acted like he had money. He didn't throw it around stupidly just because he had enough to do it. In fact, he lived conservatively and invested a lot of what he made working through The League.

She bet this cost *a lot,* even if the trip itself had been her mother and father's. That didn't mean everything else he'd factored into the trip didn't cost money. And she would not ruin it with her worries.

"We're going to Bali, Ren."

EIGHT

"Sir, we'll be arriving at the house in twenty minutes."

"Thank you."

The partition between the front and back of the car closed again, allowing Renzo his privacy from the driver.

Lush greenery, brightened by a sun so high in the bluest of skies, cloudless and *stretching so far,* had Renzo more than happy to be sitting in the backseat of a car for once in his damn life. The driver at the front had closed the partition between the front and back seats as they were chauffeured from the airport to the private residence he'd rented for the week, but the back windows were down.

Just a crack, not much.

It was enough, though.

To smell the air.

The island.

All the water.

Usually, he'd be the one in the front seat driving. He preferred that, really, because he didn't like giving someone else control of a vehicle. Today, he didn't have a single damn to give because not only did he have the best view of the volcanic mountains, thick with lush forests ahead of them, but also of the woman napping in his lap.

That flight?

So long.

Lucia had done her best to stay awake for most of it, not wanting to miss a thing. He knew that feeling, but at the same time, he didn't blame her when she'd finally fallen asleep in the seat next to his after the plane had landed and she'd snuggled in close. He was used to staying up for hours on end, constantly. Forty-eight hours with eyes peeled wide open was fucking nothing for him because that was one of the first things The League had ever taught him to do.

You have no limits.

He couldn't forget those words.

He didn't.

Drifting his fingertips through the length of Lucia's dark hair, smoothing out the strands with each stroke, he finally took his attention away from the views outside to admire the one in his lap. Those long lashes of hers fanned against her skin, and her lips stayed in the pout of her sleep, making her pretty features far softer.

She looked *happy.*

Relaxed.

And wasn't that everything he wanted?

God, he hoped this week gave his girl everything she didn't even know that she needed. Lucia worked nonstop—was still the most motivated person he knew, frankly. She woke up with a smile and went to bed with one, too. It was one of the reasons he loved her the most. You know, next to literally everything else about her.

Sometimes, he wondered if they took nearly enough time for one another in their very busy lives. Hell, there were times when he felt as though they barely even saw each other. He'd just get back from one job for The League only to be immediately sent out on another. Sure, he could refuse them, being he was an independent contractor for them now ... but he didn't know how to slow down.

Lucia never told him to.

She worked damn hard, too.

He never told her to stop.

Of course, then he had moments like these. *Quiet moments.* All he had to do was stare at her—the world seemed a little slower around him—and all he seemed to think about was that he could do this exact thing for the rest of his fucking life with her.

Absolutely nothing.

Just stare at her.

Maybe that was the thing.

Life wouldn't slow down.

He had to make it do it.

• • •

"Oh, *wow.*"

Renzo grinned, helping a still sleepy-eyed Lucia from the back of the car. He didn't mind that she wasn't really looking at him, but only because she was so entirely entranced with the vacation home waiting for them. Protected by a large, stone fence and a wrought iron gate that didn't even creak when it opened to let their vehicle into the circular driveway, it was quite a place. Deep within the forested land of the island, the three-level home had been designed with just enough of a modern hand but with a touch of the island that housed it.

The place welcomed them with a wrap-around terrace for the bottom and second floors, a cobblestone pathway, and shrubbery native to the island as they headed for the house. Because of the photos he'd seen of the place, he knew they would find scenery worth dying over, a massive pool, the waterfall he told Lucia about, a hot tub, and far more behind the place.

It was going to be a *damn* good week.

"Where are our bags?"

"Already carried in," he explained, "something else you slept through, babe."

Her hand smacked his stomach, but he only laughed. Dragging her closer to his side, he pressed a kiss to the top of her head as they climbed the stairs to the front door that was already opened and waiting for them.

"The cook comes tomorrow," he explained, "and a maid will be here later to note anything we might want ready for the next couple of days."

She grinned up at him, not even paying attention to the foyer of the large vacation home because she was far more interested in him. "Oh?"

"Yep."

"So that means—"

Renzo slammed the door behind them, saying at the same time,

"It's just us here, babe. And I know the first thing I want to do."

Her smile turned more sinful.

Playful.

"And what's that?"

"Well, I was told your parents rented this house for the pool and we both know all you have under that dress is a pair of white panties, so ..."

She cocked a brow.

He winked right back.

"Race you," she whispered.

That was all she said before darting away from him. It wasn't like she needed direction on where to go. A good portion of the downstairs seemed to be an open-floor plan and they could see from the front almost to the back. There, a wall of glass waited, acting as a window to the terrace that wrapped around the back in natural, wood tones.

He chased after her, their laughter coloring up the quiet house.

Time to give it some fucking life.

Their kinda life, anyway.

Renzo watched Lucia make it to the back of the house, where she pushed open the sliding glass doors leading to the rear terrace. Bamboo poles with a thatched roof overhead led the guests of the house straight out to the pool under the cover of shade. The terrace covered the full length of the house, too, with spots to lie in the sun, or under hammocks with similar coverings as the one he stood under while he watched Lucia drop her dress at the edge of the pool.

Her panties followed the same path.

Fuck.

He was stuck between staring and appreciating this beautiful place around him, just as much as he was captured by the raw sexiness that was his wife in her naked glory *standing here.*

Well, his wife won his attention over the island. That was okay, he thought as he headed toward Lucia just as she jumped from the edge into the clear, blue water. He'd have plenty of time over the next week to enjoy this place and all it had to offer.

First, though?

He was going to *love* that woman here.

Renzo wasted no time dropping his pants and standard white T-shirt to the ground. His boxer-briefs quickly followed the same path. His clothes on the smooth wood of the terrace were quickly soaked by the oncoming ripple Lucia made as she went under the water again and moved farther out toward the far wall that was nothing but glass overlooking the rear property.

He barely even felt the iciness of the water when he broke the surface of the pool. He was far too caught up in making it to his wife in four long arm strokes. Shaking the water from his face and ruined hair as he stood straight in the pool, he closed the distance between him and his wife where she stayed leaning against the far wall.

Her hands were already reaching for his cock when he pressed into her, their lips melding together in a familiar kiss. His thick groan from the fast strokes of her tight grip burst against her lips. And when she opened that sweet mouth of hers, he was so fucking happy to get a taste of her on his tongue.

He was enjoying her hand on his cock a little too much, but he knew it was going to be far better once he was buried deep in her pussy. Her tongue slashed alongside his as he pulled her hand from his length, stepping in between her widening legs at the same time.

Lucia let him lift her to the wall, and as fast as she got those thighs wrapped around his waist, was the time it took for him to be sliding into the heaven that was her pussy.

He still didn't feel the cold water.

Couldn't, when they were like this together.

All of Lucia's sweet sounds became muffled by the kiss he couldn't seem to break. And he loved the way her lips trembled against his when she came closer and closer to her peak.

Welcome to Bali, he thought.

What else waited for them here?

NINE

There was something … *entrancing* about a place like Bali. Maybe it was the sights from every window. Lucia stood at them to stare outside, seeing lush green trees, clear streams of water that trailed from the waterfall behind the house, and beautiful skies overhead. It could have been whatever she was breathing in because all she wanted to do was keep every single window in the large house open. The distinct scent of *island air.*

Clean.

Fresh.

Enticing.

Bali was nothing like the city, and the thing was … Lucia hadn't even left the house yet. Two days on the island and the only things she had seen so far were the house and the land it rested upon. Which honestly, were quite the sights in and of themselves.

The animals in the morning.

Palm trees swaying with that gentle breeze, bringing along a cooling wind that she enjoyed so very much to help with that heat. Oh, she certainly could have shut all the windows and appreciated the central air in the house, but what was the good in that?

She was *here.*

She just wanted to experience it.

Currently, however, she was trying to get as much information from her father as she could, but the man wasn't helping her in the slightest.

"Daddy—"

"Lucia, you're supposed to be on *vacation.*"

"And I would enjoy it far more if Aunt Kim would just pick up the phone."

Because *yeah* ... as much as she tried to just enjoy this vacation and the chance to have zero responsibilities and stress, her mind kept going back to New York and all the work she'd left behind there without any direction whatsoever. Not that her aunt couldn't handle it. Kim certainly could because hell, that gallery had once been hers. And yes, while she knew all those things very well, it still bothered her more than she could explain.

Still, Lucia hated being out of the loop.

She needed all the info.

"Listen, if I can talk to Kim—"

"She's not picking up the phone for you because she knows this is supposed to be time for you to get away from it all," her father said, his tone brokering no room for argument. She knew right then and there that he would not be helping her out here. "And that's what you're going to do, Lucia. Let her handle the gallery for the whole *week* you're going to be gone. This time away should be *relaxing* for you, *dolcezza.*"

Right.

The problem with that, though?

"I don't know how to *not* think about work, Daddy."

"Guess you better learn, hmm?"

God.

That didn't help at all.

She was sure he knew it, too.

"Thanks for nothing."

"Oh, stop, Lucia. Everything is fine here. If something were wrong, Kim wouldn't hesitate to call you."

Lucian chuckled and the sound of her father's amusement made her smile, even as she tried to keep her voice down. She wasn't entirely sure where Renzo currently was in the large house, but she had no doubt he wouldn't appreciate the fact that she was hiding in the walk-in closet of the master bedroom to use the goddamn phone.

"And hey," her father added, "does Ren know you're on the phone? Because I'm sure he told your mother and me that he planned to hide those for the week so you could both focus on this time away, right?"

Lucia scowled, eyeing the doorway. "Not sure if he knows or not …"

"And why is that?"

"Because I found where he hid the phones, and now I'm hiding from him so that he doesn't know I'm on them. No big deal."

"Lucia!"

"I'm worried about work!"

"The gallery is fine," Lucian replied, "and that is the last time I will tell you. Unless something happens, don't call me again. *Enjoy yourself,* as your husband wants you to. That man went through a lot of trouble to get this last-minute vacation set up for you both. Take the time to … do something. Sleep in more, eat food you've never tried, take more walks … *whatever.* You deserve it and so does he. You're worrying for nothing. I love you, *bambina,* and I will see you when you get home."

"Daddy—"

"I said what I said."

He didn't even give her the chance to respond before he hung up the call. Lucia was left standing in the empty walk-in closet—they hadn't brought along nearly enough things to actually use the space—staring at the phone in her hand. She had enough sense to at least turn the phone off entirely and place it back on the top shelf of the shoe rack in the closet. She put it with Renzo's, where he'd clearly thought she wouldn't go looking for it.

Nonsense.

She looked everywhere.

A whole lot of good it'd done, too.

She might have found the phones, but she hadn't gotten what she'd wanted from them. It was like despite being in this beautiful place where she should be having the time of her life, the universe still wanted to laugh at her.

Or maybe …

Maybe she should just do what her father said.

And follow Ren's lead.

Lucia gave one last look at the shelf where Renzo had hidden the phones and decided that would be the last phone call she made while on this island. *Yeah*, she would still worry about everything happening back home and with the gallery. That was just who she was, and she certainly wouldn't apologize for it, but there was nothing she could do, either.

Enjoy her time.

So, she would.

Lucia went in search of Renzo—when she'd left him earlier in the kitchen, he'd been going over the menu for the next week with the chef—but quickly realized he was no longer worrying about the food. In fact, her husband looked as though he didn't have a single care in the world as he walked along the far edge of the pool with bare feet at the back of the house.

It kind of looked like he was walking on water. The far edge of the pool was nothing more than a glass wall with a ledge that was about five inches wide. The water of the pool went right up to the top of the ledge, though, giving it that invisible appearance. It seemed to drop off into the backdrop of dense forest, framed by a waterfall a good hundred yards away, before dropping down from a ledge made up of sharp rocks into a crystal-clear pond of water down below.

One of her most favorite parts of the vacation home. Renzo's too, she knew.

For just a moment, Lucia stayed back in the shadows of the sliding glass doorway leading out to the rear terrace that Renzo had left open so she could watch him without being seen. He stopped in the middle of the ledge, a good ten feet on either side of him before he would be safely back on the terrace.

Not that it seemed to bother him.

One wrong step and he'd fall thirty feet below to the ground.

She didn't worry about that happening at all.

Besides, she was far too interested in the way her husband looked in nothing but loose-fitting pants that only reached above his ankles in length, resting low on the hard cut V of his groin. His tattooed back was on display as he stretched his arms high above his head.

He truly was a beautiful man.

And she was the lucky bitch who had his whole heart.

"Enjoying the view?"

Lucia grinned at Renzo's question, walking forward a bit until she was finally in view through the doors. Still, her husband didn't turn around to look at her. She wasn't exactly surprised that he'd known she had been watching him.

It was like the man could just feel it.

"It's a very *nice* view," she replied.

He did glance over his shoulder, then, dark eyes nailing her to the spot as he cocked a brow in challenge. "*Only* nice?"

"Best view on this island, Ren."

"Hmm, well, we'll see about that. Are you done sneaking the phones from me?"

Goddamn him.

"How did you—"

"I just know you, baby."

Right.

Lucia sighed, leaning against the sliding glass door and folded her arms over her chest. "And what are you doing out here, anyway? A whole *one with nature* bit, or …?"

"Thinking. And also waiting for our car."

"What?"

"A car," he repeated, "we're going out."

"To do what?"

"How about you just enjoy the day, huh?"

Lucia smiled. "That sounds perfect, Ren."

He shrugged, still holding her stare and making her heart skip beats. Even thirty feet away, he could still look at her and make her feel like the only woman in the world for him.

"Thought so. Get a dress on that you can move in, Lucia."

She didn't need to be told again.

TEN

"Okay, now this is how we should eat *everyday.*"

Renzo grinned, nodding. "Absolutely."

Lucia winked at him where she sat across the small table they currently dined at under a hut that was set a good thirty feet off from the restaurant. They had to walk to it on a path made of smooth rocks. She shoved another bite of rice into her mouth.

Part of the draw for the restaurant was the fact that one could dine either inside, or outside, in private, under one of the many huts that surrounded the place. Reservations for this place hadn't been on the docket, but after chatting with the chef who worked at the house, the guy said he could pull some strings if Renzo made it worth his while.

Ren did.

Worth every penny of that thousand dollars.

Lucia loved it.

The soft tempo of a song reached their spot. A tune that could make anyone want to dance, though there were no lyrics. Although where it came from, Renzo couldn't be sure. Nonetheless, the music had Lucia swaying to and fro across from him, the delicate line of her shoulders moving to the beat of the song while she finished what was left on her plate.

"I need another drink," she said, picking up her empty glass and waving it at him. "And you need to give me a dance."

"Oh, you think?"

"Mmhmm."

"Which do you want first?"

Because he wasn't entirely sure where their server went, but it seemed as though there were only a couple that worked the huts outside. Not that he minded because it allowed them more time to enjoy the place together, without worrying about someone coming to interrupt them every few minutes. Besides, he could easily go in and find a server to bring them out another round of drinks.

He didn't mind.

Lucia eyed her glass carefully, and then her gaze darted to him over the rim. "That's a *very* hard decision, Ren."

His smile grew wider, and his tongue peeked out to lick the corner of his upper lip as he asked, "Is it really?"

"These are good drinks, but you're a good dancer, so …"

"Think maybe you've had one too many drinks."

Lucia shook her head. "Not nearly enough, actually."

Right.

God, he loved this girl.

"One more drink," he said, "but I thought you might want to see the Ubud Art Market, and we can't do that if you're so drunk that you can't walk."

Lucia pursed her lips, her index finger coming up to tap at her chin while she stared at the ceiling of the hut and considered his words. "*Well …*"

"Hmm?"

"You have a point. Maybe water would be better."

Renzo let out a quiet laugh, because *yeah*, he didn't need her to admit it for him to know exactly how buzzed she was feeling. Hell, after three of his own drinks, he felt it. Neither one of them was driving, so that wasn't a problem. He just knew the market was something she would appreciate the most about Bali, next to the obvious beauty and magic of the place. He doubted she wanted to miss out on it because she had one too many drinks.

"Water first, then a dance," he told her.

Lucia sighed. "*Fine.*"

Renzo leaned back dangerously in the chair, letting it dangle on two legs as he peered around the support beam of the hut to see if maybe the server was on his way back. Unfortunately, not from what he could see. "Stay put, hmm?"

"Where would I go, Ren?"

"Never know with you, baby."

Her guffaw followed him out of his chair, and he gave her a kiss on the top of her head as he passed her by to leave the hut. Renzo didn't bother looking for a server when they really didn't need one whole person just to bring them out two glasses of something to drink. Instead, he headed for the bar and ordered from the woman there. She didn't seem to mind.

The bartender had just put the glasses to the counter when a phone in Renzo's cargo shorts started to buzz. *Again.* It'd been doing that all day—so far—and the only reason why Lucia had yet to notice was pure luck, and perhaps a bit of the fact that she was really enjoying herself.

He felt like a *shit.*

His regular cell phone and hers were both put away—shut down and done for as long as they were still on this vacation and no emergency came up. That was their deal. Thing was, Renzo couldn't shut off *one* of his phones, and as Lucia hadn't asked about *this* phone, which had been provided by his bosses at The League, well ... he didn't offer the information.

And today, that phone rang.

And *rang.*

Not once had he'd bothered to pick up the calls but only because he wasn't required to. Besides, Dare and Cree both knew he was away on vacation, so why someone from The League decided to call his phone was beyond him.

However, just to make sure they didn't keep calling, Renzo pulled the phone out of his pocket while he was in the safety of the restaurant and Lucia wouldn't know. "Yeah, Ren here."

He hadn't even bothered to check the caller ID. Not that it mattered. It would only be a handful of people calling that goddamn number.

"You don't pick up the phone or what?"

Ah.

Cree.

"You know," Renzo said, "it's been a few days since I heard your voice, Cree, and it wouldn't have been a bad thing had I gone a few days more."

"That's not how you greet someone."

"And what about your attitude, huh?"

"My attitude is just part of my winning personality. Like it or don't, that's not my problem."

And that was Cree in a nutshell.

As fun as this was—and it wasn't fun at all—Renzo was ready to get back to his wife and their vacation. He still had plans for the rest of their day, and he intended to make sure she enjoyed every single bit of it. She wouldn't do that, however, if he was on the phone with people who needed to learn to respect his time.

"Listen," he started to say, "I am on vacation, and everybody knows it. So, I'm not sure why you are calling this number—"

"Dare needs a favor."

Renzo stilled. "I beg your pardon?"

Cree cleared his throat. "You heard me."

"No, I'm sure I *didn't*. At least, not correctly."

A sigh echoed through the speakers.

Renzo waited the man out because *shit* ... maybe he had heard him exactly right. It wasn't like Cree or Dare to ask for anything like a favor, but especially not from one of their members. They weren't the people who *owed* debts, they collected them and made others pay up for them. They trained assassins, and then lorded it over them for the rest of their lives.

"Shit luck, I guess."

"What?"

Because Renzo hadn't been paying attention.

He probably should have, though.

"Were you even listening to me?"

"You want honesty?" Renzo asked.

Cree grunted under his breath, muttering, "*Listen.*"

"I am now."

"An … old friend of Dare's," Cree said, "owns massive properties in Bali, one of which is a hugely popular resort for tourism on the island."

"All right. What's that got to do with this favor?"

"The guy has a son—sixteen years old."

"*And?*" Renzo demanded.

Because he felt like he was missing something here. Or was that just him?

"The father … he called a couple days ago. Said his kid had gone missing. Except he hadn't really gone missing; that's just *rich people* bullshit for *my kid is mixed up with the wrong people, and my money won't get me out of the problem.*"

Renzo's brow furrowed.

Cree sounded … annoyed.

"You okay?"

"Fine, why?"

"Nothing, just—you sound pissed."

"That my husband's ex wants us to take his kid from a gang and train him as a League member? Oh, and Dare is willing to go ahead with it because he feels like he owes that fuck something. Yeah, that kind of pisses me off."

Renzo blinked.

Five times.

Because that's how long it took him to absorb everything Cree just told him. Oh, sure, he'd heard *rumors* about Dare and Cree. Things like the two men were more to each other than just members of the same organization. He'd once asked Alessio Sorrento—another League member—about it, seeing as how Cree and Dare had basically taken the guy in and raised him from the time he was ten, but Les never said one way or another.

"Uh—"

"Sorry, that was a bit more info than I meant to give," Cree said thickly. "Just … the kid is sixteen, and not only is he wanted by the authorities there for some of the dealings he's had with this *gang* … but now his father hasn't had contact with him for over two weeks. He's willing to pay a lot of money to have the kid protected and straightened out."

"Straightened out, huh? That's a nice way to say you're going to break him on every level possible and make him wish he were dead."

"Yeah, well, I don't make the fucking rules."

There was that attitude again.

"You've got the week to figure it out and we'll help with the details," Cree said, "but basically you're going to have to put him on a plane. That's the gist of it. *Easy.*"

"But is it?"

"Pardon?"

"Easy," Ren clarified. "Is it easy?"

"No. It never is."

Right.

"I have to get back to my wife," Renzo said. "Call after one in the morning—this is supposed to be mine and Lucia's time. At least if you call around that time, this won't affect her."

"Will do. And uh … thanks, Ren."

"Yeah, but you all owe me."

Cree made a disgruntled noise. "*Dare* does. Have him pay up."

Oh, he certainly would.

ELEVEN

Lucia couldn't help but run her fingers over the strokes of oil paint that made up the sunset and beach portrait the artist had painted on a smooth piece of wood carved in the shape of a surfboard. It wasn't a *one-of-a-kind* design, considering there were twenty other painted miniature surfboards right beside it, but that didn't matter to her.

It was still amazing.

All the attention to detail.

"That's all you want for this?" she asked the man behind the small booth who had previously given her the price.

One that was far too low for the time put into this.

He gave her a look. "Ma'am, people tend to barter *lower* in the market. It's how things are done."

She couldn't imagine that.

"I don't barter with artists," she explained quietly, her attention going back to the foot-long surfboard painting in her hands, "because I feel like they know what their art is worth and who am I to tell them differently?"

Even if that was her job ...

That never mattered.

Lucia's respect for art was unmatched in that regard, and without artists who could make a livable income on their work, then there wouldn't be *anything* for her to admire and appreciate. She wouldn't have a goddamn job, either, without people willing to make art for her to show off, celebrate, or sell.

"No need to barter," she told him, smiling.

She understood that it was a tradition here, and even Renzo had warned her about it when they'd first stepped into the market later in the afternoon—*everything will be a higher price because we're later in the day*, he'd added—but she couldn't do it. Bartering wasn't in Lucia's blood, but frankly, she was happy to pay the price the man originally asked.

Which she did.

He offered a brown paper bag to wrap her treasure in, but Lucia refused, fine to carry the item through the market for now. Besides, once she found where Renzo had gone, it was only around the corner at a shop selling T-shirts and musical instruments that the two of them had broken away from each other, he could hold her painted surfboard.

There were quite a few more things in the market that she wanted to check out, but not without Renzo keeping her company. Plus, she needed his arms to carry all the things back to the car, and he was so good at doing that.

Lucky for her, she didn't have to search long. In fact, he hadn't even left the shop with the T-shirts and music. Only now, as she stood in the doorway looking in, she found that her husband didn't seem as interested in the clothing or whatever else the store was selling.

A little girl had caught his attention.

The brown-eyed, black-haired girl looked to be no more than five, if that. Maybe even younger. And yet, she was having the time of her life, dancing on the tips of Renzo's combat boots while he held her hands and a man sat on a nearby stool, strumming out a fast tune on a guitar. A woman next to the man wearing a loose-fitting, flower-printed dress clapped in tune, her smile wide and her gaze fond as she watched the two.

Maybe the girl's mother.

Lucia had no idea.

Although, as fast as she noticed the other people in the shop, Lucia was quick to go back to the sight of Renzo dancing with the little girl. It wasn't just the child who seemed as though she were having the time of her life.

Renzo was loving it, too.

She hadn't expected to feel *something* stirring in her stomach and chest at the sight—something new; a feeling she had never given much thought to before now. But watching him dance with that little girl, his smile so fucking wide, reminded her of how good a father he would be. That all the love he kept so close to his chest because that's just who he was deserved to be shared with someone else in their life. Yeah, they had Diego, and Renzo often volunteered when he had the time for the youth centers in the city, but none of that was the same, she knew.

It wasn't *their* child.

It wasn't lost on her in that moment how Renzo had never once asked that of Lucia. They'd talked about kids, yeah, and what they wanted, but he never said it needed to happen. And he certainly didn't put a time limit on it. He didn't make demands or constraints, almost like he was waiting for *her* to decide when the time should be right for them.

Was the time right now?

Did they have time in their already busy lives for something like *babies*?

She didn't know.

When was it ever the right time?

Not that it mattered.

She heard the clock ticking *now.*

Loud and clear.

Funny, how something like that could change in a second.

The man playing the guitar brought the song to a close with applause from everyone in the shop, and Renzo, too. Even Lucia joined in, which finally seemed to catch her husband's attention and let him know she was there waiting for him.

He gave her a wink.

She blew him a kiss right back.

The little girl stepped off his toes and beamed up at him. "Thank you for helping me practice my English, Mister."

"Thank you for that dance," her husband replied.

And there went her heart.

Melting into a puddle.

He said goodbye to the little girl, paid for the items that he had sitting on the floor next to where they'd been dancing, and then he joined Lucia in the doorway. For a second, she just stared at her husband as he slipped both arms around her waist and pulled her close enough that he could tip his head down and drop a soft kiss to her lips. Between them, she held tight to the painted surfboard.

"Found someone to dance with, did you?"

He shrugged. "Didn't know where you were."

"Mmhmm, well, I'm not *that* jealous about it. It was terribly cute."

The grin he flashed her was downright sinful. "Oh, are we back to me being *cute*, baby?"

"Well ..."

"I can always remind you why I soar far beyond cute."

"Not here, you can't," she replied.

She was sure they still had an audience, even if she was too caught up in her husband to notice the rest of the people.

Renzo made a face. "Mmm, maybe not."

Before Lucia lost her nerve, she asked the thing that was waiting on the tip of her tongue. "Do you want a baby?"

He tipped his head to the side, a small smile curving his lips in the sweetest way. "You know the answer to that, Lucia."

"Yeah, I know you want kids. I meant ... do you want them *now?*"

That made him pause.

She waited him out.

"I just ... was waiting on whenever you were ready for that," he said quietly.

"Yeah, that's what I thought."

"And we're always busy."

"We can't slow down a bit?"

Renzo arched a brow. "Babe, I can do anything for you."

Yeah.

She knew that, too.

"So, let's slow down."

He dropped another kiss to her lips, although this one lingered just long enough to make her forget about the market entirely. "Let's slow it down, Lucia."

TWELVE

Renzo lingered in the master bathroom's doorway while Lucia finished her nightly rituals. Mostly cleaning away the makeup of the day, pulling her hair back to secure it while she slept, and putting that melon-smelling moisturizer that made her skin *so fucking soft* all over. It also made her taste even more edible, not that he was supposed to know how the lotion tasted, but that was a story for another day.

Then, she'd brush her teeth.

Which she had.

And take her pill.

Her birth control pill.

She'd gone back and forth between a few different methods of contraceptive, always letting him know when she switched to something else to try so that he could be extra careful. The pill seemed to be the one thing that didn't bother her as much hormonally, as she had less mood swings, didn't gain weight, and wouldn't have to deal with annoying shit like breakouts. Not that he cared about any of those things, but *she* did. So, the pill it was and whatever made her happy was just fine for him.

Tonight, she didn't take the pill.

"You were serious about that, then?"

She peered at him over her shoulder. That towel she'd wrapped around her form after getting out of the shower slipping slightly, but she didn't bother to fix it. He was hoping that soon, the towel would be gone altogether. Matter of fact, he seriously hoped she left it right where she stood before leaving the bathroom, seeing as how he was already hard from standing there watching her get ready for bed … *naked.*

"Hmm, what?"

"The *baby* thing."

"Why would I joke about that?"

Renzo shrugged. "Never said you were joking—just thought maybe you may have thought about it a little more and changed your mind. I'm never really sure what goes on in that mind of yours, babe, not unless you let me in on all the secrets."

"Ren."

"Yeah?"

"I don't change my mind that easily."

Right.

She told no lies.

"So, that means what I think it means, then?" he asked.

Lucia's lips split into a grin that felt entirely sinful as she helped the slipping towel along by pulling it away from her body completely. That left her in nothing but silky, gleaming, gold skin under the soft lights of bathroom. He had the best view of the curve of her waist and the way her lower back melded into a pert, round ass.

Fuck, yeah.

"That means what you think it means, Ren."

His tongue peeked out to wet the seam of his lips as she walked toward him. "Love you, huh?"

"More than you know."

Oh, he knew.

He'd know it forever.

When she was close enough for him to grab and drag close, he did just that. Once his lips crashed with hers, the world around him exploded in two things—*sensation* and *need*. Both of which warred together, their similarities too much and just enough to make him so fucking selfish to get those things from her.

"God, you better fuck me good, Ren."

See?

It wasn't just him who was selfish here.

"You know I love that—don't you? When you just *demand* I fuck you?"

Lucia smiled slyly. "Of course, I do."

Which was why he made it worth her while for the next hour as he sated the greedy side of himself. He made sure she came when she was on her knees. Flat on her back, too, and even bent over the bed. He gave her what she needed, and then he took his time to slow their chaotic love down when he rolled over to let her ride him to his own release.

God.

He loved this woman.

• • •

Renzo took a moment to admire the sight of Lucia curled up in the white sheets on the bed where she'd rolled over to his side the very second after he'd gotten up. There was nothing he wanted more than to sit and stay right there with her, but the time was ticking closer and closer to one in the morning with every passing second, and he didn't want to be anywhere near her while he chatted about this *thing* he had to do for The League in Bali.

Besides, she needed to sleep.

Especially after their day and night.

Knowing if he didn't go right then that he would stay there and watch her until his phone started to vibrate, Renzo headed into the hallway. Taking the stairs at the end two at a time—his footsteps still as light as a feather against the shiny hardwood floors—he headed for the back of the house. He had just gotten his laptop booted up on the back terrace while the sleeping forest whispered all around him when his cell phone vibrated on the glass table.

He didn't hesitate to pick it up.

"Yeah, Ren here."

"Wondered if you were going to decide to tell me to fuck off for this favor."

His brow raised at the voice on the other end of the call. He expected it to be Cree, considering that was who called him in the first place. It was Dare, instead.

"Hear you got a problem with an ex, huh?" Ren asked.

Dare made a harsh noise.

In the background, Ren heard a familiar voice bitch, "Could we *not?*"

Ah, there was Cree.

"Let's ignore that bit," Dare said quietly, "someone is a little sour about it."

"Because you were so fast to say *yes* after everything that asshole—"

"You all can call me back after you settle whatever issue you've got going on, you know?"

Dare sighed. "No, it's fine."

"Right, well—"

"It would be better for all of us," Dare quickly explained before another issue could start, "if the officials from Indonesia, as well as the United States, weren't in Banyu's business, considering the ties that man has to *many* criminal organizations around the world— including mine. Before his little issue, meaning that kid of his, starts to cause more problems than he already has, we will fix it."

"*He* has more than enough money to fix the issue without asking you, Dare."

Cree clearly wasn't pleased.

"Would you knock—"

"It's a way for him to worm his way back into your life, nothing more."

"There's a viable threat to The League by way of exposure, and I can't risk that, Cree."

Cree snarled under his breath.

Great.

They were back to this again.

"How about," Renzo said, "I will get the kid, once you two let me know how I should do that, then I'll deliver him to where he needs to go, and the rest of you can work out your fucking issues on your own time, yeah?"

Silence answered Ren back.

He didn't mind that a bit.

"Well?" he asked after a moment.

"How many men do you think you'd need to extract the kid?" Dare asked. "From the source his father has, the kid is located in Kuta—not far from where you are. A little bit of money shoved into the right hands, and we can easily nail down his exact location."

"Cree said he's mixed up with a gang?"

"Yeah, apparently."

Renzo nodded, though the men couldn't see it. He'd already pulled up Google maps, and was currently scanning them, but he currently didn't have much to go on so it didn't particularly help. "Three men, including me, to be safe. I want *full* get up for this—bulletproof vest and all. A mask, too, so make sure it's all on hand for me."

"Let us get the kid's location nailed down first."

"Call me when you do—*after* one in the morning."

"All right." Dare let out a slow breath. "And thanks, Renzo."

Right.

"Thank me when I ask for it—*how* I ask for it."

THIRTEEN

"So, you've got, what, two more days there?"

Lucia smiled at her brother on the screen, nodding. "Yep."

"Can't wait!"

In the background of the video chat, Lucia watched as Diego passed by the chair John was currently using. She wasn't at all surprised to see the kid at his house, considering John and Siena—plus their kids—lived only a couple of blocks away from Rose, her husband, and Diego. The teenager often went to John's place to hang out, play games, or just do whatever. And John was happy to keep an eye on him.

For whatever reason, Diego didn't take as easily to his sister's spouse as he did for … well, Lucia, when she'd come into Renzo's life.

Renzo blamed the fact that Diego had been a lot younger when Lucia had come around, and he hadn't been the type to be jealous back then. Rose's husband came along when he was twelve, they married shortly after he'd turned thirteen, and he was still trying to adjust to this man—who, Lucia thought after meeting and spending time with him, was quite kind, and loved Rose to death—who took up a lot of his sister's time, and was now the head of the house.

They didn't fight.

Diego didn't … cause problems.

Neither did Rose's husband, considering the man didn't even discipline Diego. He left all that up to Rose and Renzo, and never said a word edgewise about it. It was clear he cared a lot about Diego and tried to give him space, but something was still there.

A tension was *definitely* there.

They were working on it.

"How's he been the last week?" she asked, lowering her voice when she saw in the corner of the screen that Diego had left the kitchen area. "He hasn't been able to talk to Ren too much, so I wondered if maybe—"

"He's doing fine."

"Oh, well, good."

John shrugged. "Sometimes, you have to give teenagers a bit of time to work out whatever thing they're going through. It's not like adults can understand, you know? Stuff that seems petty or silly to us might mean their entire lives are ending."

"Bit dramatic."

"And that's exactly my point. You have to at least try to see something from their perspective if you want to understand why they react the way they do. Things would go a lot smoother, in that case."

Yeah.

She supposed he might be right. Not that she would admit it out loud. If she did, her brother's ego would grow, like most men's, and that would be yet another thing Lucia would have to deal with. Today was not the day for that. Tomorrow didn't look great, either.

"He talked to Ren this morning," John said.

"I know, for like an hour."

"He misses him."

Clearly.

They missed everyone at home, too.

"Besides, I heard he *couldn't* talk to Ren," John added, "because someone decided you all needed to turn off your phones and just enjoy your vacation, huh? What happened to that, seeing as you're on here, chatting with me right now?"

Lucia grinned. "You're not wrong."

"*So?*"

Damn her brother.

"We might have come to the mutual conclusion this morning that both of us are homesick like nothing else. We're not used to being so unplugged from everyone—at least not *willingly* like this. Renzo has to leave his phone behind when he takes a job, but that's different. Anyway, we wanted to call and say hello to some people."

John put a hand over his chest, a smile splitting his lips as he faked a happy sigh. The bastard even dared to lean back in his chair and stare upward like he was thanking God or something. "And I was just lucky enough to be one of those *people.* I love you, too, Lucia."

She laughed.

The *ass.*

Truth be told, though, her brother was still her very best friend. She had lots of girlfriends, a ton of family, and Renzo, too. Yet, at the end of the day, it was still John she called when she wanted to gossip or just needed to talk. It'd taken them a while to get back to that place with one another, but she hadn't minded at all when it came to putting in the work between them. She loved her brother to the very ends of the earth and back.

She knew he loved her the same.

Even when he drove her *crazy*.

After all, what was family for?

"Anyway," John said, "we're all looking forward to seeing you both when you get back. Siena, especially, wants to take you out to breakfast, so make sure you put aside a bit of time for her, yeah?"

Lucia almost rolled her eyes—her brother, forever his wife's biggest protector, even if Siena didn't know it and didn't need it.

"I will make time for her, I promise."

"Good. Enjoy the rest of your vacation. Bring me home something."

"Like you did for me when you went to the—"

"Love you, bye, kiddo."

John hung up the call with a grin and a wink that said he knew exactly what he was doing. That was all Lucia saw as the call cut off, too. Just her brother's frozen face in that smug expression before the screen went back to the home page of the video chat app altogether.

Fucker.

She still loved him, though.

Lucky him.

As she didn't have anyone else to check in with—she'd already called her parents, and her other siblings, as well as her assistant, although *only* to tell the woman she was going to need a couple of extra days after her vacation before she returned to the gallery—Lucia powered down the laptop and put it away.

Then, she went in search of Ren.

Soon enough, she found him in the outdoor shower, surrounded by walls made of smooth rocks on the upper terrace that they could use privately by walking through the sliding doors from the master bedroom. The showerheads dropping water on him looked like small waterfalls, and for a moment, Lucia stood back and enjoyed the sight of her husband's naked, wet body. All those hard lines of his dripping with rivulets of water, and his muscular legs shifting from foot to foot as he wiped the wetness from his face.

Renzo turned, shaking the droplets from his face at the same time. His gaze came to land on her just beyond the shower. She didn't move to join him, although she would soon. There was little to no doubt about that. If only because she had no self-control around this man, and now he was *grinning* at her like he knew it, too.

Goddamn him.

She loved him.

"How's everyone?" he asked, reaching for the bottle of shower gel sitting on the floor.

And *yeah* ... that gave her a nice side view of his ass.

A very sexy ass.

"They're good—missing us as much as we miss them."

Ren nodded, standing straight again with the bottle in his hand. "And then you know like a week after we're gone, we'll miss Bali, right?"

She didn't doubt it.

"We'll come back," she replied.

"Yeah, we'll come back."

His gaze drifted over her form, his stare lingering in all the right spots and making her wish she were under the shower with him. He tipped his head back, that silent invitation she'd been waiting for. She didn't even hesitate to join him.

FOURTEEN

Learning to walk without making a single sound could be unsettling to most people around him, but Renzo found it to be a valuable asset. Like now, he moved around the bedroom in the Bali vacation home without his wife as much as shifting on the bed. She slept peacefully while he gathered things he needed, between his bags in the walk-in closet and the phone still stuffed in his discarded jeans from earlier.

He'd already dressed—waited just long enough for Lucia to fall into a deep sleep before doing so. He wore all black from his head to his toes, which was the standard uniform whenever he did a job for The League. It was one of their first lessons. A man needed to learn how to blend in, even if he was the type to stand out in a crowd.

He couldn't draw attention.

Turning the device provided by The League on, he took a moment to appreciate the sight of his wife, who was happy and unbothered on the bed. He liked to believe that she'd found a good head space here. All the stress of life that she'd left behind in New York probably didn't seem like such a mountain now; more like a small hill for her to tackle.

That's all he wanted.

Knowing damn well it was about to be a long night for him, he crossed the bedroom and dropped a kiss to the top of his wife's head before smoothing back the wayward strands of her hair that had fallen in her eyes during sleep. Her lips curved into a soft smile, and while he couldn't be sure if that was from him or whatever she was dreaming about, he also figured it didn't matter. As long as she stayed happy, then that's what counted.

"See you soon, babe," he murmured. "I'll be back—promise."

Forever.

He'd always come back.

It was one of her greatest fears, and while she didn't voice them, that didn't make it any less real to Lucia. She'd told him all of *once*, and he'd listened well enough to know that she wouldn't tell him each and every time that he went out on a job. It wasn't like the fear was unfounded, either, considering how dangerous his line of work could be.

And still, he came back.

He made sure of it.

Dropping one more kiss to her forehead, Renzo straightened to his full height and left the bedroom without another look back. He had to. Otherwise, he might never leave at all. Her fear might revolve around his safety, but his was firmly stuck in the idea that he *had* to go when he never seemed to want to.

Win some, lose some.

Life was funny like that.

Renzo gathered the other things he needed as he walked through the house and headed for the front entrance—his lighter on the counter, the pack of cigarettes he'd left near the back of the house, and even the small sleeve inside the hidden compartment of his bag that had a fake ID, cash, and a passport.

All things he needed *just in case.*

Stepping out of the house through the front, he found two black vehicles already parked and waiting in the circular driveway. He'd passed the code for the gate onto Cree, who'd then given the information to whatever team would be helping him here with this little side project for The League. Between the two cars, six men stood waiting.

More than he needed.

Renzo would take it.

"Someone's gotta stay here," he said, taking the steps two at a time, "but whoever it is, they don't go into the house and the woman inside *never* sees you. Got it?"

None of them said a thing.

They all nodded, however.

Yep.

All in all, should be an easy job.

• • •

Feeling like he might finally have enough miles put between him and the city of Kuta to be considered safe, or as close as he was ever going to get, Renzo pulled the black mask from his face. He'd have to put it on again before transferring his ward at the next checkpoint to make sure his face wasn't seen, but he would deal with that when the time came. All things The League demanded. He'd also like to yank off the goddamn bulletproof vest that felt a little too tight around his chest, but *shit* ...

One thing at a time.

The thumping in the back of Renzo's vehicle had finally come to a stop but seeing as how he was *so fucking exhausted* and within three hours the sun would be high in the sky, it might be the fact that his brain had just shut off and wasn't hearing anything.

But who was he to say?

The Bluetooth in the car beeped through the speakers as the call he had been trying to make for the last thirty minutes—man, there was some shitty service in different parts of the island, unfortunately—finally picked up on the other end.

"Is it done?"

That's all Cree asked.

Renzo let out a slow breath, his gaze darting to the rear-view mirror to check the road behind him. There, the second black car in his team traveled terribly close to his bumper. Not that he found that problematic, seeing as he had told them to follow that close.

"Yeah," he finally said, "or mostly. Traveling the kid to the boat now—it'll take him off the island and then they'll get him to the private jet out of—"

"Yeah, I know. No problems?"

"Not particularly. Bunch of guns came out when we went into the spot where he was staying with the gang. Man ..."

"What?"

"He's a *kid*, Cree. Just—"

"A bit younger than I normally train, yes."

Renzo cleared his throat. "He seemed scared."

"He should be."

Right.

That couldn't be forgotten.

"Everything from here should be standard, yes?" Cree asked.

"By all accounts, the hard part of this is done."

"Mmhmm, well, the boy's father called Dare earlier. Said to make sure we told his son—Taman, in case you forgot—that this is for the best."

Renzo didn't believe that for a second. Having been the person that boy was currently in the trunk of his car, taken from a bad situation and put into the care of The League, then trained to become this ... *thing*. This person—an assassin who killed for a dollar amount—was not always the best thing, but now wasn't the time to argue about it, honesty.

He had better things to do.

Places to be after he left here.

Like back with his wife.

"I'll call you when I hand the boy off at the next checkpoint," Renzo said dryly.

"You sound—"

"Goodbye, Cree."

He ended the call before the other man could respond.

It didn't make a difference that Renzo ended the call so he wouldn't have to keep talking about the situation with the boy in the back of his trunk. The forty-five minutes that he had to drive to the drop-off point were more than enough time for him to go over every last detail that bothered him. Or rather, made him nervous for the kid.

Once he got to The League, Ren knew what would happen and how it was going to go from there. Nothing about this was easy. Frankly, he wasn't sure he wanted to be someone who *delivered* someone to that fate, either.

Oh, well, he thought, staring up at an inky sky while the road came a little faster at his vehicle. *You're almost back home with your wife.*

Even if Bali wasn't home.

Nor was that vacation house.

Lucia, though?

Well, wherever she was, that's where his home would be.

He just wanted to get back there.

FIFTEEN

When Renzo was home—not out on a job somewhere in the world—it was rare that Lucia woke up alone. And by rare, she meant it literally never happened. However, that last morning in Bali, when she blinked awake in the soft sheets, the first thing she realized was how empty the bed felt next to her. Sure enough, when she turned to check, Renzo's warm body wasn't next to hers. By the looks of the smoothed sheets, he hadn't been there most of the night.

She took a minute.

Then, two.

Just to blink away the sleepiness in her eyes and the sensation of dreams still lingering in her mind. She took in her surroundings, stretched out under the white sheets, and breathed in the island air that floated in with the breeze from the window that had been left open the night before next to the bed.

Still, she kept looking to Ren's side of the bed and how empty it seemed without him being there to wake up with her in the morning. She didn't like that at all, so as much as she wanted to stay right there in the comfortable bed and maybe get another hour of sleep before she had to start packing to leave the island, she got up and went in search of her husband. After, of course, she made a pitstop in the bathroom to take care of her morning business and splash her face with some cold water to wake her up even more.

Lucia didn't even bother to take the time to change into something other than the over-sized T-shirt of Renzo's that she'd stolen the day before to sleep in. There was something she loved about stealing his clothes to wear when she could—they smelled like him, kept her warm just because, and gave her a sense of home like nothing else but him could do. Sometimes, she swore he left her a T-shirt he'd worn for a day at the bottom of their bed right before he left for a job, just so that she would have a fresh one while he was gone.

It didn't take Lucia long to find her husband on the back terrace, and she wasn't at all surprised that's where he'd gone. It seemed to be his favorite spot in the whole house, considering the many things he found to do back here between the pool, the forest he liked to explore, and the many sitting areas.

Including the one he currently used.

A square hammock attached to large wooden beams stretched out from the side of the terrace, hanging over … well, nothing but air, really. Thirty feet down below was the lush greenery of the forest and foliage, but the hammock itself simply hung out into the air, giving the person lying in it the appearance and sensation of free floating.

And that's where her husband rested.

With an arm flung over his face, turned half on his back and half on his side, one might think he was sleeping because of the rhythmic rise and fall of his chest. Lucia knew better, though, because she saw that soft smile curving his lower lip beneath his arm. His grin grew a little wider as she approached him, letting her know he was awake despite his position. She couldn't help but wonder what about this hammock was more comfortable than sleeping in bed with her.

Not that she was offended.

Ren had strange ways sometimes, and she had simply become accustomed to rolling with the punches, so to speak. He occasionally still slept in a bathtub when shit was extra stressful, or he had something on his mind that he didn't really want to talk about.

Eventually, she would find him wherever he hid away, and he'd tell her all the shit keeping him quiet and inside his mind. She figured, if that's what this was, then the same thing would happen. It was something they did time and time again—his *thing*—and she never complained about it one way or another. That was something she'd learned about love a long time ago, and she thanked Renzo for teaching her that, too.

You had to love the whole person.

Oddities and flaws included.

"Morning," she said, coming to stand next to the hammock. "The bed wasn't good enough for you last night or what?"

A chuckle echoed from the man in the hammock. "If only, babe."

"Hmm?"

Finally, he pulled his arm away from his face to give her a better view of him. He grinned up at her, and Lucia couldn't help but smile back at him. His arms opened to her, inviting and far too tempting for her own good. And *damn* ... didn't he look so fucking good below her with that sexy grin, his fingers wiggling to urge her forward? He was like her own personal little devil sitting on her shoulder, whispering about sin and how *good* it would be.

"Come here, would you?" he asked.

How could she say no to that?

Well …

She couldn't.

Lucia kneeled down before climbing into the hammock and Renzo's waiting embrace. She didn't typically like the sensation of floating that the hammock provided, but while she was wrapped in his arms, nothing else mattered but this right here. The world went away, and so did the rest of the stresses and problems she faced.

She snuggled against his chest, burying her face into his warm scent. The black T-shirt he wore wasn't what he had gone to bed in the night before, and neither were the black jeans that rubbed against her bare thighs. She didn't bother to ask about those things because for one, she didn't care, as long as he was holding onto her, and for two … well, sometimes it was better not to ask when it came to Renzo.

She never knew what the answer might be.

"I wanted to be in bed with you," he said, his words whispering along her hair after he'd tucked her head into the crook of his neck, "but you know how *wants* go, huh?"

"No, I usually get what I want, actually."

Renzo's chuckles echoed all around them. A dark, lovely sound that affected Lucia in the best way, and even overtook the noise of the forest and waterfall that usually gave them a nice soundtrack to relax to when they were outside. She liked the sound of him far more.

She always would.

"I'm trying to tell you something here, Lucia."

She tipped her head up, perfectly happy to remain hidden from the world while she used Renzo to do it, but some things were just more important than what she wanted. "And what's that, exactly?"

"I had a job last night."

She blinked. "What?"

"Just what I said, babe," he replied.

"And you didn't tell me? I thought Bali was—"

"Just a vacation, and it was. *Still is.* It was a last-minute thing," he said with a sigh, "and given how simple it seemed—I had it done in a night, and you didn't even know the difference—I didn't want to refuse when it was a favor, anyway."

Huh.

"Still could have told me, Ren," she whispered.

"Why, so you would worry all night that I might not come back?"

Lucia opened her mouth to deny that.

Renzo gave her a look that kept her quiet.

"I would have tried really hard *not* to do that," she told him.

"Exactly, and that's not what this trip was about."

"Is that why you're all in your feelings out here in the hammock, instead of waking me up in bed like you usually do?"

He smiled. "You know me too well."

"Of course, I do, Ren."

"Anyway," he said, his words barely above a murmur as he tucked her back into his embrace and tightened his hold just enough to make her shiver, "I came back—like I promised."

Right.

Yeah.

That's always what mattered.

EPILOGUE

Two months later …

"Ren, what has you calling me? I thought you were taking a year sabbatical from—"

"I am," Ren interjected before Dare could continue speaking, "and maybe even longer, but we'll see how it goes."

"Hmm, I hear people around here might actually *miss* your special brand of arrogance, but who am I to say?"

And they could keep missing him.

For now.

"Anyway, why the call?" Dare asked.

Ren dragged in a quick breath, settling the sudden nerves he felt making themselves known. It wasn't like him to get *nervous*, but here he was. It also wasn't like him to give a shit about some stranger—a kid from an island that he barely spoke more than a handful of words to—but here he was doing that fucking nonsense, too.

Maybe the kid reminded him of his brother.

Maybe it was something else …

Shit, maybe Ren just *cared*.

"The kid—Taman—from the Bali job a couple months back. Uh, how is he?"

Dare quieted for a minute.

Longer than Ren thought was normal.

"All things considered; he's adapted well to training. Bit of an attitude, but we're used to that here, and even you learned to tamper it after a while."

"Is he out of phase one?"

The dark room.

The fucking *tank*.

"As of three weeks ago, yes," Dare replied. "Something you want to tell me, or …?"

"No, I just—"

"Felt the need to check in. It happens."

"Does it?"

Dare let out a slow breath. "Sometimes. You know, a long time ago, I thought I could raise men and women in this organization to be … individuals without feelings. It would be for the best, considering the work you all do."

"And?"

"You're all still very human."

Dare almost sounded *proud* of that fact.

For whatever reason …

"I'll probably check in on him again," Renzo said.

"Feel free, and you're always welcome to come to Vegas to check in directly, you know?"

"I'll keep it in mind."

But no promises.

He only made those to his wife.

Speaking of which …

"Ren!"

Lucia's shout from upstairs brought him back to reality, and far away from the phone call. He quickly said goodbye to Dare and hung up the phone. Setting the device to the counter, he didn't even bother taking it with him as he headed for the upper portion of their brownstone. He figured his wife would be in their bedroom, as that's where she liked to spend the majority of her morning when it was one that she didn't have to go to the gallery first thing.

Instead, he found her in the bathroom.

With a pregnancy test.

Ren froze in the doorway.

Lucia smiled as she turned the test around for him to seeing the blinking word on the digital screen spelling out the one thing they'd been waiting for since that Bali trip. It hadn't happened the first month, but they weren't too worried about it, considering she'd *just* stopped her birth control. He didn't know if it would happen on the second month, but apparently, they were just lucky enough that it had.

PREGNANT.

"*Look*, Ren," she whispered.

"I see it—I see it, babe."

Each word he spoke took him one step closer to her until he had her in his arms, and that test was hidden between them.

"Love you, love you so fucking much, Lucia."

She hugged him back even tighter. "Love you, too, Ren."

It was time to start another piece of their forever.

He couldn't wait.

ABOUT THE AUTHOR

Bethany-Kris is a Canadian author, lover of much, and mother to four sons, two cats, and three dogs. A small town in Eastern Canada where she was born and raised is where she has always called home. With her boys under her feet, a snuggling cat, barking dogs, and a spouse calling over his shoulder, she is nearly always writing something ... when she can find the time.

Find Bethany-Kris at her:

WEBSITE: www.bethanykris.com
BLOG: www.bethanykris.blogspot.ca
FACEBOOK: www.facebook.com/bethanykriswrites
TWITTER: @BethanyKris
INSTAGRAM: www.instagram.com/bethany.kris
PINTEREST: www.pinterest.com/bethanykris

Sign up to Bethany-Kris's New Release Newsletter here:
http://eepurl.com/bf9lzD.

OTHER BOOKS

Renzo + Lucia

Privilege
Harbor
Contempt
Forever

Andino + Haven

Duty
Vow

John + Siena

Loyalty
Disgrace

Cross + Catherine

Always
Revere
Unruly
The Companion
Naz & Roz

Guzzi Duet

Unraveled, Book One
Entangled, Book Two

DeLuca Duet

Waste of Worth: Part One
Worth of Waste: Part Two

Standalone Titles

Dirty Pool
Effortless
Inflict
Cozen
Captivated
Dishonored

Donati Bloodlines

Thin Lies
Thin Lines
Thin Lives
Behind the Bloodlines
The Complete Trilogy

Filthy Marcellos

Antony
Lucian
Giovanni
Dante
Legacy
A Very Marcello Christmas
The Complete Collection

Seasons of Betrayal

Where the Sun Hides
Where the Snow Falls
Where the Wind Whispers
Seasons: The Complete Seasons of Betrayal Series

Gun Moll Trilogy

Gun Moll
Gangster Moll
Madame Moll

The Chicago War

Deathless & Divided
Reckless & Ruined
Scarless & Sacred
Breathless & Bloodstained
The Complete Series
Maldives & Mistletoe

The Russian Guns

The Arrangement
The Life
The Score
Demyan & Ana
Shattered
The Jersey Vignettes

Find more on Bethany-Kris's website at www.bethanykris.com

www.ingramcontent.com/pod-product-compliance
Lightning Source LLC
Chambersburg PA
CBHW051306170626
46809CB00004B/1785

* 9 7 8 1 9 8 8 1 9 7 9 7 5 *